**DATE DUE** DEC 04

GAYLORD

PRINTED IN U.S.A.

# Gone Forever!
# Iguanodon

**Rupert Matthews**

Heinemann Library
Chicago, Illinois

Customer Service  888-454-2279
Visit our website at www.heinemannlibrary.com

Designed by Ron Kamen and Paul Davies and Associates
Illustrations by James Field of Simon Girling and Associates
Photo Research by Rebecca Sodergren and Ginny Stroud-Lewis
Originated by Ambassador Litho Ltd.
Printed and bound in China by South China Printing Company

07 06 05 04
10 9 8 7 6 5 4 3 2

**Library of Congress Cataloging-in-Publication Data**
Matthews, Rupert.
  Iguanodon / Rupert Matthews.
     p. cm. -- (Gone forever!)
Summary: Describes what has been learned about the physical features,
behavior, and surroundings of the long-extinct iguanodon.
Includes bibliographical references and index.
  ISBN 1-4034-3657-6 (hardcover) -- ISBN 1-4034-3668-1 (pbk.)
  1. Iguanodon--Juvenile literature. [1. Igunaodon. 2. Dinosaurs.] I.
Title.
  QE862.O65M34 2003
  567.914--dc22
                        2003012297


**Acknowledgments**
The author and publishers are grateful to the following for permission to reproduce copyright material: p. 22 Museum of Brussels, Belgium; pp. 4, 6, 8, 10, 12, 13, 18, 20, 24, 26 Natural History Museum, London; p. 16 Science Photo Library; p. 14 Senekenberg Nature Museum/DK.
Cover photograph reproduced with permission of the Natural History Museum, London.

Special thanks to Dr. Peter Makovicky of the Chicago Field Museum for his review of this book.

Every effort has been made to contact copyright holders of any material reproduced in this book. Any omissions will be rectified in subsequent printings if notice is given to the publisher.

# Some words are shown in bold, **like this.** You can find out what they mean by looking in the glossary.

# Contents

Gone Forever! . . . . . . . . . . . . . . . . . . . . 4

Iguanodon's Home . . . . . . . . . . . . . . . 6

Changing Plants . . . . . . . . . . . . . . . . 8

Other Dinosaurs. . . . . . . . . . . . . . . 10

Getting It Wrong . . . . . . . . . . . . . . 12

What Was Iguanodon? . . . . . . . . . . . 14

Baby Iguanodons . . . . . . . . . . . . . 16

On the Move. . . . . . . . . . . . . . . . . 18

Run for It! . . . . . . . . . . . . . . . . . . 20

The Herd . . . . . . . . . . . . . . . . . . . 22

Time to Eat. . . . . . . . . . . . . . . . . 24

Fighting Iguanodon. . . . . . . . . . . . 26

Where Did Iguanodon Live? . . . . . . . . . 28

When Did Iguanodon Live? . . . . . . . . . . 29

Fact File . . . . . . . . . . . . . . . . . . . 30

How to Say It . . . . . . . . . . . . . . . . 30

Glossary . . . . . . . . . . . . . . . . . . . 31

More Books to Read . . . . . . . . . . . . . 32

Index . . . . . . . . . . . . . . . . . . . . . 32

# Gone Forever!

Some animals are **extinct.** This means that all the animals of that type have died out. None are left alive. Scientists called **paleontologists** can find out about extinct animals by studying **fossils.**

4

**Hypsilophodon**

**Iguanodon**

**Hylaeosaurus**

Iguanodon is an extinct animal. It lived about 120 million years ago in many places around the world. It was a plant-eating **dinosaur.** The dinosaurs and nearly all other animals that lived at the time of Iguanodon also have become extinct.

# Iguanodon's Home

Scientists called **geologists** study rocks. They look at the rocks in which Iguanodon **fossils** have been found. These rocks can tell geologists about the place where Iguanodon lived.

teeth

rocks containing
Iguanodon teeth

The land where Iguanodon lived was warm. Plenty of rain fell. The land rose and fell in low hills. Rivers ran along the bottom of shallow **valleys.** Forests covered most of the land, but there also were some open areas. Many Iguanodon fossils have been found in areas that used to be **marshes.**

7

# Changing Plants

**Paleontologists** have found **fossil** plants in the same rocks as fossils of Iguanodon. This means that the plants grew at the same time that Iguanodon lived. Some of these fossils showed a completely new type of plant. This new type of plant had flowers.

**fossil leaf of an
early flowering plant**

Before the time of Iguanodon, none of the plants on Earth had flowers. The first plants with flowers were small and grew in damp places in **valleys.** Today, plants with flowers grow all over the world.

# Other Dinosaurs

**armor plates from a Polacanthus**

Scientists have found **fossils** of other **dinosaurs** in the same rocks as Iguanodon fossils. One of these dinosaurs was Polacanthus. Scientists have found fewer fossils of Polacanthus than of Iguanodon. This means it was probably not as common as Iguanodon.

Polacanthus was about as long as a family car. It ate the leaves and shoots of plants near the ground. It had large spikes and tough bone **armor** along its back. These gave it protection against meat-eating dinosaurs.

# Getting It Wrong

**Fossils** of Iguanodon were some of the very first **dinosaur** bones ever found. At first, only some teeth were found. Then people discovered some leg bones, a thumb spike, and a few ribs. Scientists were not sure how the bones fit together.

In 1854, scientists built this model of Iguanodon. They thought it looked like a rhinoceros, and they put the thumb spike on its nose! Since then, scientists have found more Iguanodon fossils. Now we know better what it really looked like!

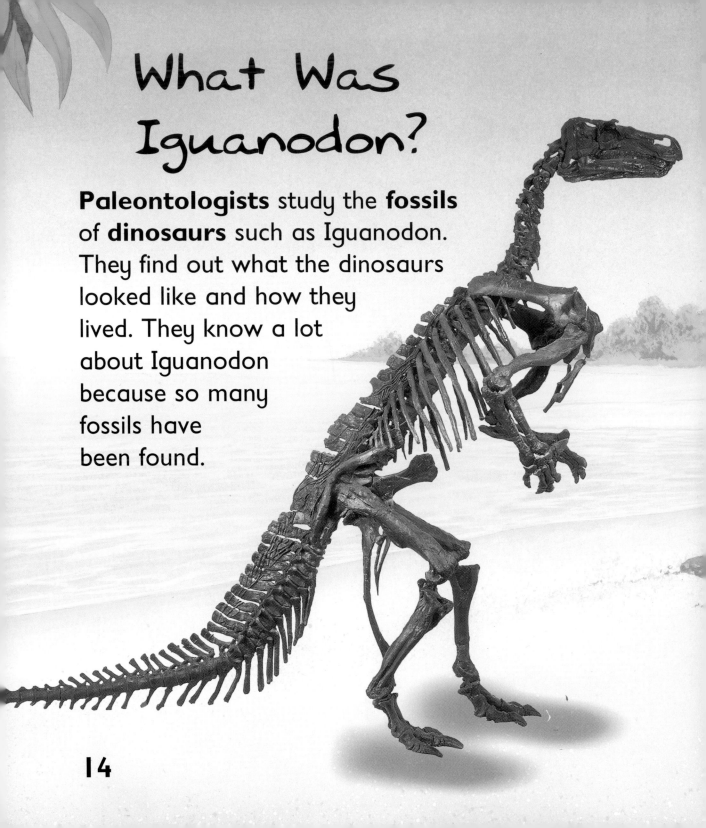

# What Was Iguanodon?

**Paleontologists** study the **fossils** of **dinosaurs** such as Iguanodon. They find out what the dinosaurs looked like and how they lived. They know a lot about Iguanodon because so many fossils have been found.

14

Iguanodon was about as long as two minivans parked end to end. Its teeth show us that Iguanodon ate plants. The bones show that it was very strong and could move fast.

# Baby Iguanodons

**Paleontologists** have not found any Iguanodon eggs or **fossils** of babies. But perhaps young Iguanodons **hatched** from eggs laid in nests of mud and leaves. The young were probably about as long as your arm when they hatched.

**dinosaur eggs**

The babies may have stayed in the nest for several weeks. The mother Iguanodon probably brought them food to eat. When the young were large enough to take care of themselves, they left the nest.

# On the Move

The **hind** legs of Iguanodon were strong and **muscular**. The hind feet had three toes. The front feet had five toes. Three of the toes ended in small **hooves**. Iguanodon may have rested on its front legs when bending down to drink or to eat small plants.

**an Iguanodon hind foot**

18

Iguanodon probably walked on all fours most of the time. This way of walking does not use much **energy.** Iguanodon could stand up on its hind legs to reach food. It also could look around in case meat-eating **dinosaurs** were near.

# Run for It!

Iguanodon's **hind** legs were long and strong. The bones show that powerful **muscles** joined the legs to the hips. Iguanodon could walk using just its hind legs.

**Paleontologists** think Iguanodon ran on its hind legs when it needed to move quickly. Iguanodon could probably escape from powerful meat-eating **dinosaurs** this way.

# The Herd

The **fossils** of more than twenty Iguanodons have been found close together. This shows that the animals lived in **herds.** Perhaps the fossils belong to a herd of Iguanodons that drowned in a flood.

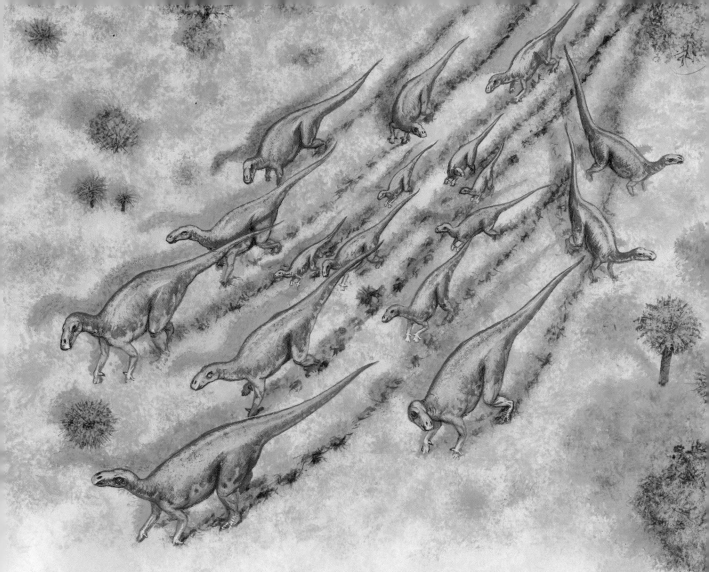

**Paleontologists** think herds of Iguanodons kept close together for safety. The grown-up animals may have stayed on the outside of the herd. They could warn the others if a meat-eating **dinosaur** was nearby. The smaller Iguanodons stayed in the center of the herd, where they were safer.

# Time to Eat

Iguanodon had jaws that were different from the jaws of other **dinosaurs.** At the front of the jaws was a sharp **beak.** The backs of the jaws were full of strong, flat teeth. Iguanodon could move its upper jaw from side to side.

beak

Iguanodon jaws

Iguanodon used its beak to bite leaves and twigs from plants. Then it used its jaws to move its teeth from side to side. This ground up the plants into a thick paste. This paste could be **digested** quickly after it was swallowed.

25

# Fighting Iguanodon

Iguanodon could use its front feet as weapons. Its thumbs were long, sharp, bony spikes. The spikes were covered in horn. They stuck out sideways from the Iguanodon's wrist.

**thumb spike**

26

Iguanodon may have used its spikes to fight off
meat-eating **dinosaurs.** Iguanodon could use its
strong **muscles** to jerk its front legs forward. This
would jab the thumb spikes into a dinosaur enemy.

27

# Where Did Iguanodon Live?

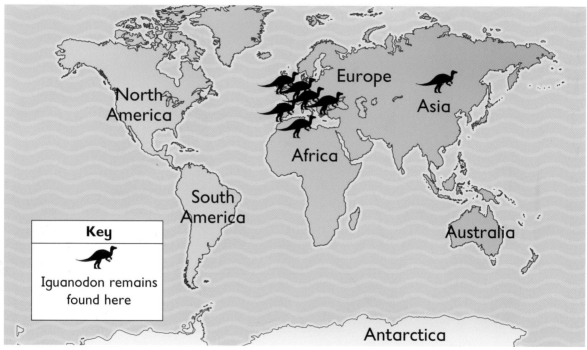

**Paleontologists** have found Iguanodon **fossils** in Europe, Asia, and North Africa. They have found fossils of animals like Iguanodon in North America and China.

# When Did Iguanodon Live?

Iguanodon lived on Earth between 125 and 100 million years ago. It lived in the Age of the **Dinosaurs,** which scientists call the Mesozoic Era. This was in the early part of what scientists call the Cretaceous Period.

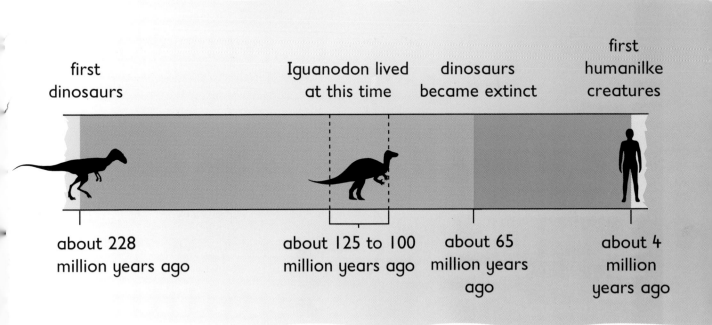

first dinosaurs

Iguanodon lived at this time

dinosaurs became extinct

first humanilke creatures

about 228 million years ago

about 125 to 100 million years ago

about 65 million years ago

about 4 million years ago

# Fact File

| Iguanodon | |
|---|---|
| **Length:** | up to 33 feet (10 meters) |
| **Height:** | up to 13 feet (4 meters) |
| **Weight:** | about 5 $\frac{1}{2}$ tons (5 metric tons) |
| **Time:** | Early Cretaceous Period, about 125 million years ago |
| **Place:** | Europe and North Africa |

# How to Say It

Cretaceous—krih-tay-shuhs
Iguanodon—eh-gwan-ah-don
dinosaur—dine-ah-sor
paleontologist—pay-lee-uhn-tahl-uh-jist
Polacanthus—pole-uh-kan-thuhs

# Glossary

**armor** hard covering of shell or bone that protects soft body parts

**beak** hard, horny covering on jaws. Birds have beaks.

**digested** describes the process that happens in the stomach and other body parts so that food can be used by the body for fuel

**dinosaur** reptile that lived on Earth between 228 and 65 million years ago. Dinosaurs are extinct.

**energy** power to do things. Animals get energy from food.

**extinct** word that describes plants and animals that once lived on Earth but have all died out

**fossil** remains of a plant or animal, usually found in rocks

**geologist** scientist who studies rocks

**hatch** break out of an egg

**herd** group of animals that live together

**hind** word that describes the back legs or feet of an animal

**hoof** piece of horn on the toes of some animals

**jaw** part of the skull that holds the teeth

**marsh** area of ground that is covered with shallow water most of the time

**muscle** part of an animal's body that makes it move

**muscular** having a lot of strong muscles

**paleontologist** scientist who studies fossils to learn about extinct animals, such as dinosaurs

**valley** low area of land between hills or mountains

# More Books to Read

Cohen, Daniel. *Iguanodon.* Mankato, Minn.: Capstone Press, 2003.

Rodriguez, K. S. *Iguanodon—Prehistoric Creatures Then and Now.* Chicago: Raintree, 2000.

Wilkes, Angela. *Big Book of Dinosaurs.* New York: Dorling Kindersley, 1994.

# Index

baby Iguanodon  16–17
beak  24–25
bones  15
eggs  16
food and eating  17, 18–19, 25
fossils 4, 6, 8, 10, 12–13, 14, 22
herds  22–23
home  5, 6–7, 28, 30
jaws  24–25

legs and feet  18–19, 20–21, 26–27
other dinosaurs  10–11
plants  8–9, 15
rocks  6
size  15, 30
teeth  15, 24
weather  7